HAUNTED PLACES
HAUNTED HOUSES

KENNY ABDO

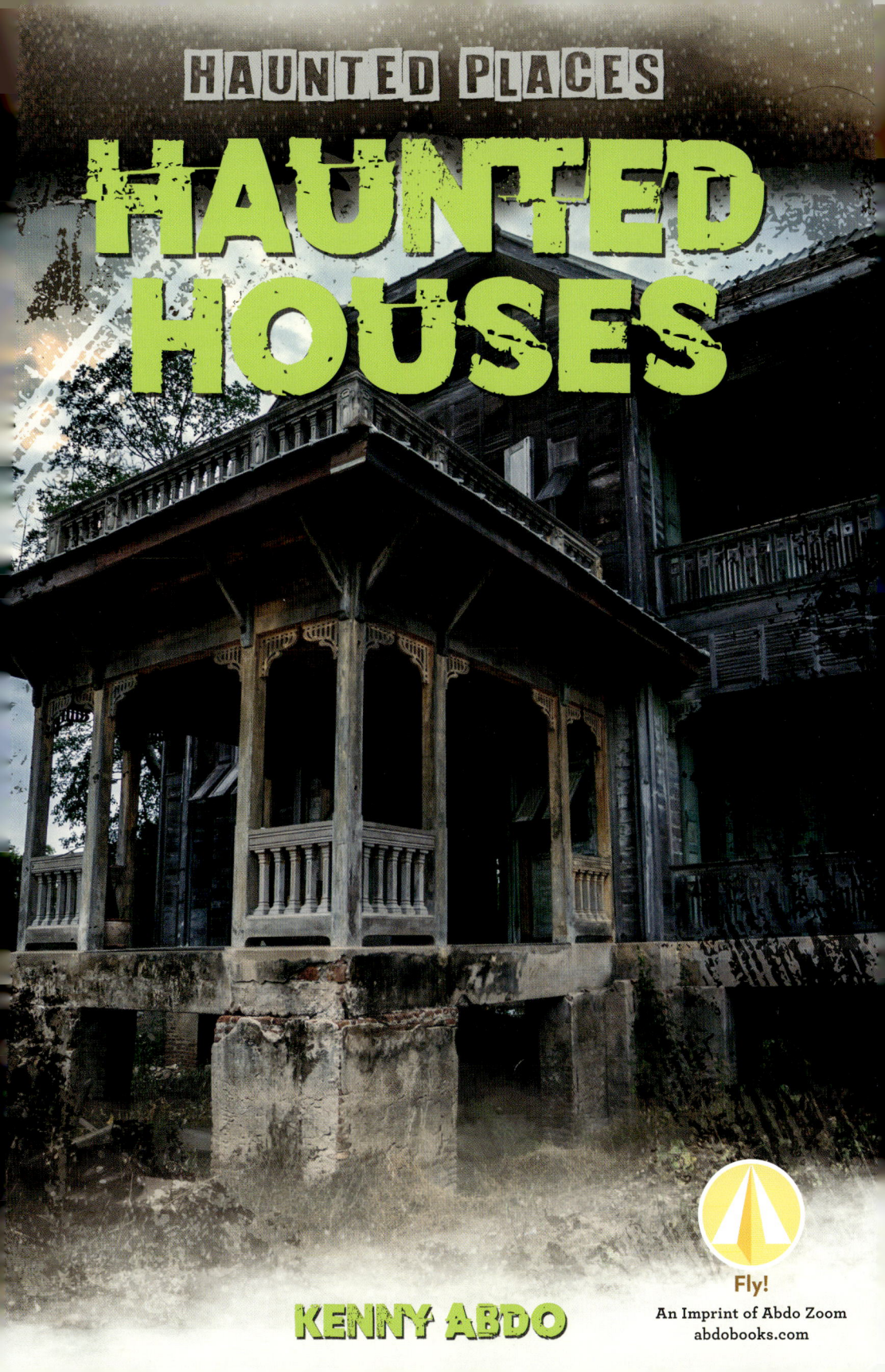

Fly!
An Imprint of Abdo Zoom
abdobooks.com

abdobooks.com

Published by Abdo Zoom, a division of ABDO, P.O. Box 398166, Minneapolis, Minnesota 55439. Copyright © 2021 by Abdo Consulting Group, Inc. International copyrights reserved in all countries. No part of this book may be reproduced in any form without written permission from the publisher. Fly!™ is a trademark and logo of Abdo Zoom.

Printed in the United States of America, North Mankato, Minnesota.
052020
092020

THIS BOOK CONTAINS RECYCLED MATERIALS

Photo Credits: Everett Collection, iStock, North Wind Picture Archives, Shutterstock, ©Aasiaat p9 / CC BY-SA 2.0, ©Beyond My Ken p13 / CC BY-SA 4.0, ©Ryan Moomey p16 / CC BY 2.0
Production Contributors: Kenny Abdo, Jennie Forsberg, Grace Hansen
Design Contributors: Dorothy Toth, Neil Klinepier

Library of Congress Control Number: 2019956159

Publisher's Cataloging-in-Publication Data

Title: Haunted houses / by Kenny Abdo
Description: Minneapolis, Minnesota : Abdo Zoom, 2021 | Series: Haunted places | Includes online resources and index.
Identifiers: ISBN 9781098221324 (lib. bdg.) | ISBN 9781644944134 (pbk.) | ISBN 9781098222307 (ebook) | ISBN 9781098222796 (Read-to-Me ebook)
Subjects: LCSH: Haunted places--Juvenile literature. | Haunted houses--Juvenile literature. | Ghosts--Juvenile literature.
Classification: DDC 133.122--dc23

TABLE OF CONTENTS

Houses 4

The History 8

The Haunted 12

The Media 20

Glossary 22

Online Resources 23

Index 24

HOUSES

As the saying goes, "There's no place like home." And that's especially true when that home is filled with tortured **spirits**.

5

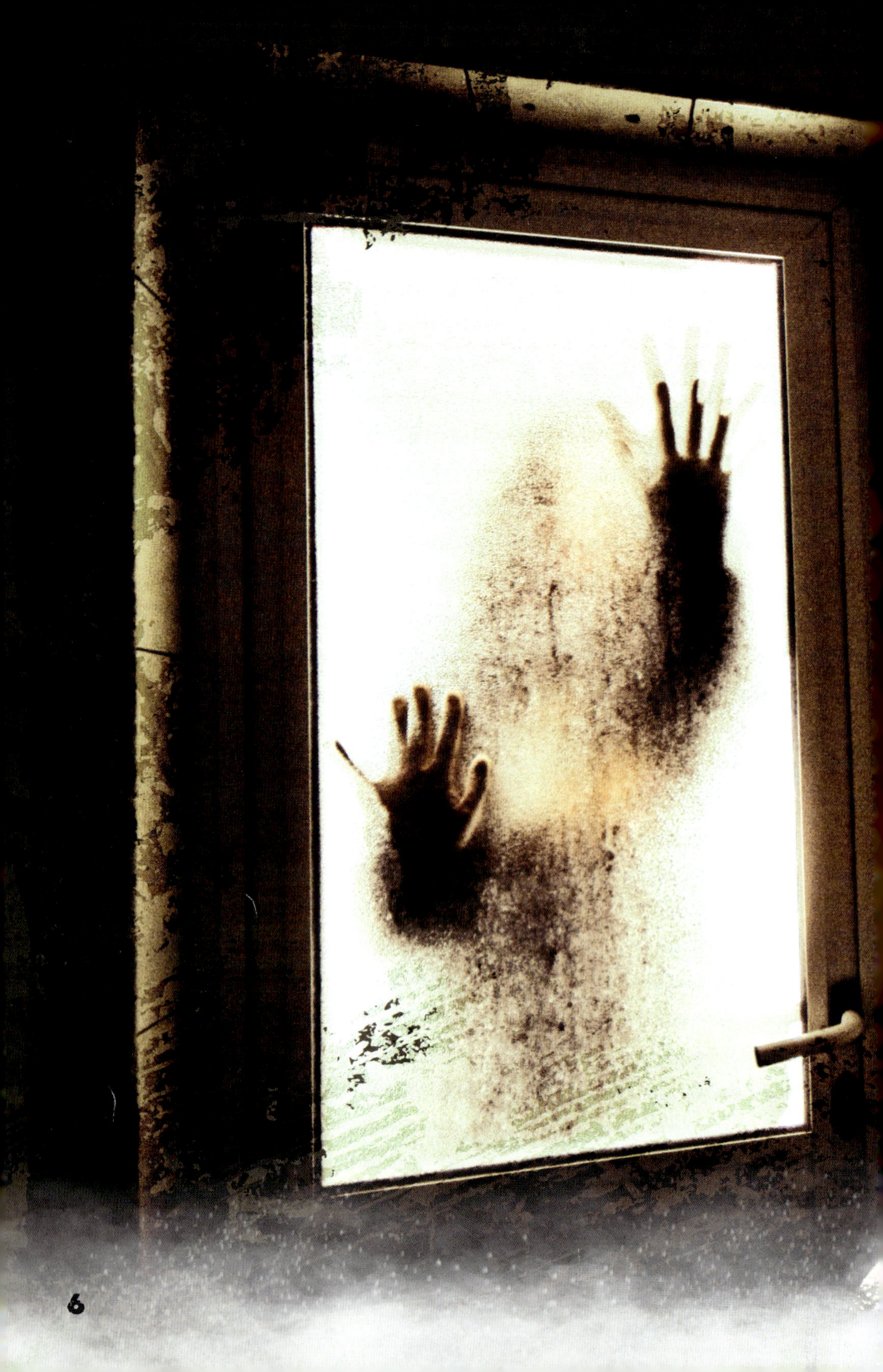

Haunted homes have been the settings of horror **lore** for centuries. Stepping into a real haunted house can spook even the bravest of people.

THE HISTORY

The word "house" comes from the Old English word *hus*. A house is a building where people live.

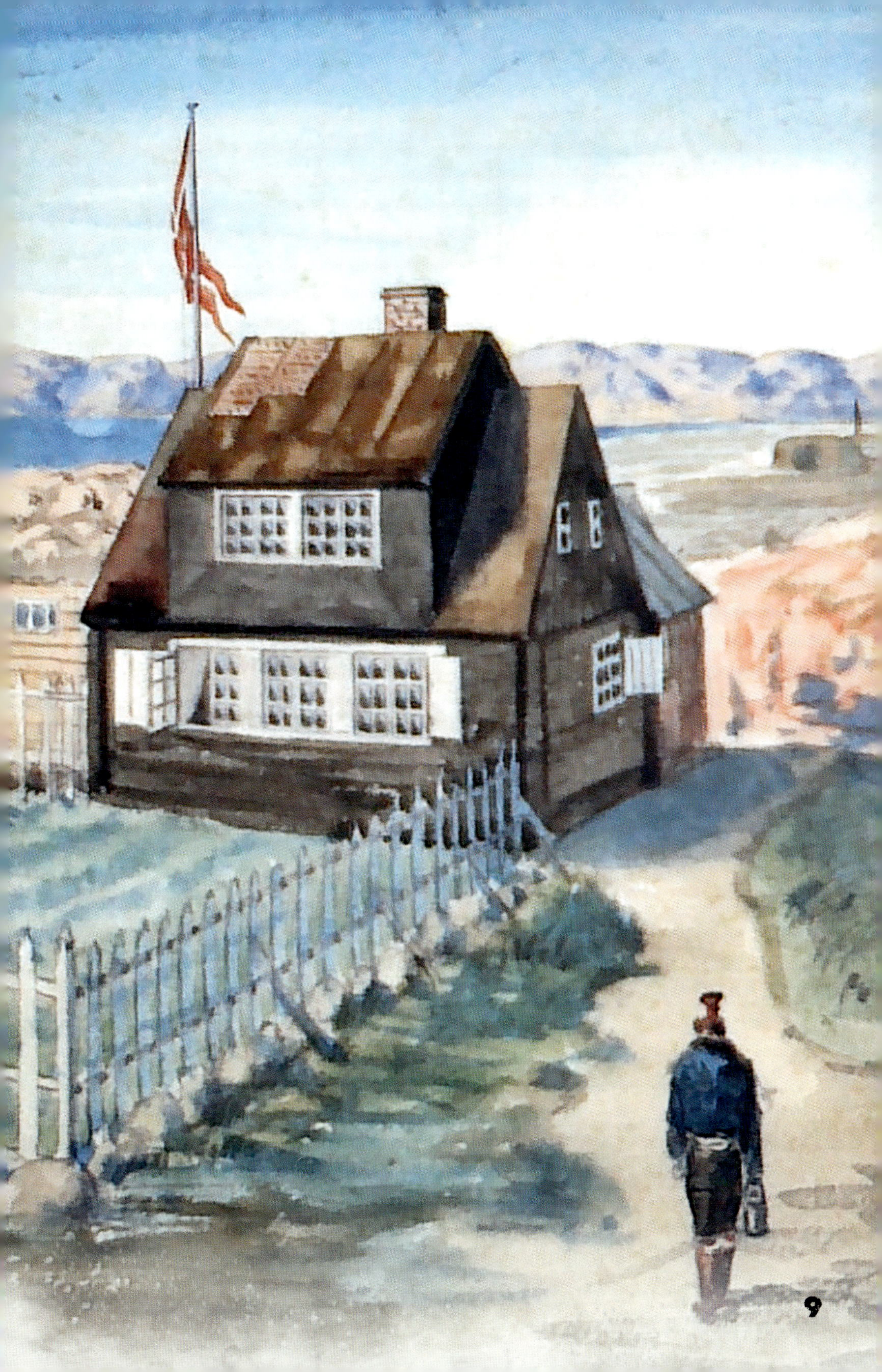

Houses can range in size from simple shacks or huts to large, sprawling mansions.

Haunted houses are usually **occupied** by the **spirits** of those who once lived there. Some may be protecting their home, while others don't even know they're dead!

THE HAUNTED

The House of Death is a townhouse in the heart of New York City. It is said to be haunted by more than 20 people. Some died within its walls. Others were frequent visitors. Some witnesses report that they've seen the ghost of author Mark Twain there.

13

Thomas and Anna Whaley built a house in San Diego in 1857. It was on the spot James "Yankee Jim" Robinson was **executed**. The home is supposedly haunted by Yankee Jim, the Whaleys, and their family dog.

The Gribble House was the scene of a ghastly crime in 1909. Locals have witnessed strong **paranormal** activity in the Savannah house. The **eerie** feeling that someone is touching you as you walk through the house is often reported.

The Villisca Ax Murders took place within the Moore Family home in 1912. People have reported the sounds of children crying coming from the Iowa home. And some have even seen a man holding an ax!

Houses aren't haunted by just ghosts. The Sallie House in Kansas is reportedly haunted by a **demon** who looks like a little girl. Owners have suffered unexplained burn marks and scratches on their bodies.

Perhaps the most famous haunted house is located at 1600 Pennsylvania Avenue.

Some of the world's greatest leaders **occupied** the White House. And some say their **spirits** still roam the halls to this day.

THE MEDIA

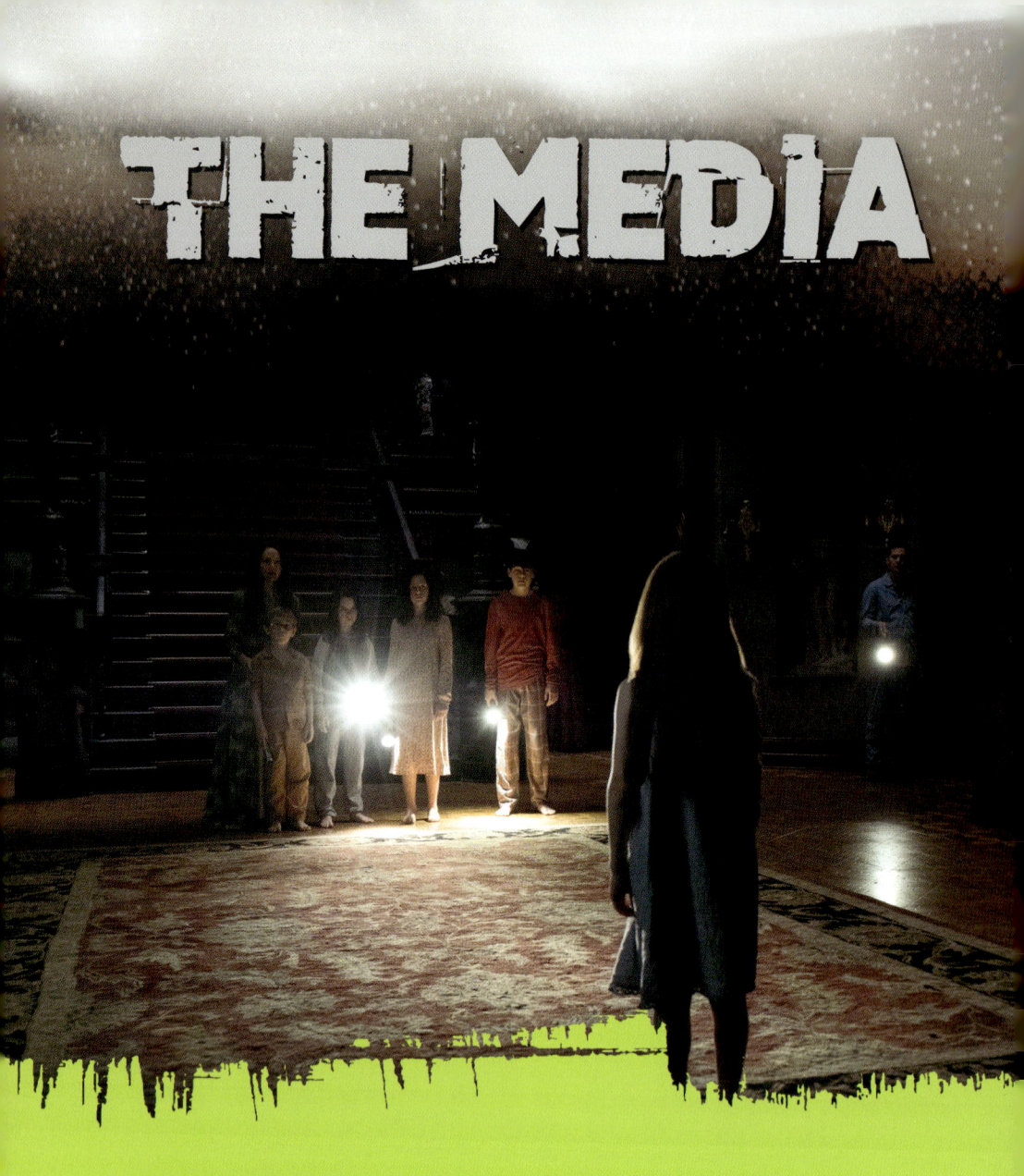

Haunted houses are the settings for several popular movies and shows. From Disney's Haunted Mansion to *The Haunting of Hill House,* Hollywood has some seriously scary real estate!

Many of these homes have beautiful architecture and a rich history. But if you come across one of these haunted houses, don't go knocking on the door.

21

GLOSSARY

demon – an evil spirit, thought to possess or torment a living person.

eerie – mysterious and frightening.

execute – to put to death by law.

folklore – a story handed down from person to person.

paranormal – an occurrence beyond the scope of scientific understanding.

occupied – lived in.

spirit – a being that is not of this world, such as a ghost. Some believe that a spirit is a force that is a part of humans that lives on after they die.

ONLINE RESOURCES

Booklinks
NONFICTION NETWORK
FREE! ONLINE NONFICTION RESOURCES

To learn more about haunted houses, please visit **abdobooklinks.com** or scan this QR code. These links are routinely monitored and updated to provide the most current information available.

INDEX

Georgia 15

Haunted Mansion (Disney) 20

Haunting of Hill House (TV Show) 20

Iowa 16

Kansas 17

New York City 12

Robinson, James "Yankee Jim" 14

San Diego 14

Twain, Mark 12

types 10

Whaley, Anna 14

Whaley, Thomas 14

White House 18, 19